As Long as the Sky is Blue

Brett Carty

ISBN-13: 978-0-9908978-0-4

ACKNOWLEDGMENT

I dedicate this book to my Father, James Carty. He always told me that he admired my imagination and creativity. I entered college with the intention of one day writing books for children and young adults. I wrote this poem at the age of 21, on a hot August night, in between preseason football practices. Unexpectedly, my father passed away three months later. I recently rediscovered this poem and I decided to illustrate it ten years later. So this is for you, Dad.

Son, as long as the sky is blue,

I will always love you.

I will teach you the alphabet
letter by letter,

I'll help you put on
your favorite striped sweater.

The sun will shine with quiet divine

while we cast a fishing line.

Thunder and lighting will shake you with fright,

but I will protect you with a hero's might.

School will come with pencil and lunch bag,

and gleeful games of schoolyard tag.

Then sports with bat and ball,

and you won't listen to me much at
all.

But I will be there from small to tall,

and I'll always catch you when you

fall.

You'll grow up and forget me,

but when you have a son you'll see,

that I am more than a distant

thought,

for you'll remember all I taught.

But most of all remember this one
thing,

no matter what else you've learned
under my wing,

Son, as long as the sky is blue,

I will always love you.

ABOUT THE AUTHOR

Brett Carty was born and raised in the Philadelphia area. He received a B.A. in Archaeology from Wesleyan University and an M.A. in Geography from West Chester University. Among other things, he loves comic strips, maps and books.